This igloo book belongs to:

...................................................................

# igloobooks

Original story by L. Frank Baum
Retold by Melanie Joyce
Illustrated by Eva Morales

Cover designed by Lee Italiano
Interiors designed by Justine Ablett
Edited by Hannah Cather

Manufactured in China. FIR003 1017
10 9 8 7 6 5 4 3 2 1

Library of Congress Cataloging-in-Publication
Data is available upon request.

ISBN 978-1-4998-8007-6
IglooBooks.com
bonnierpublishingusa.com

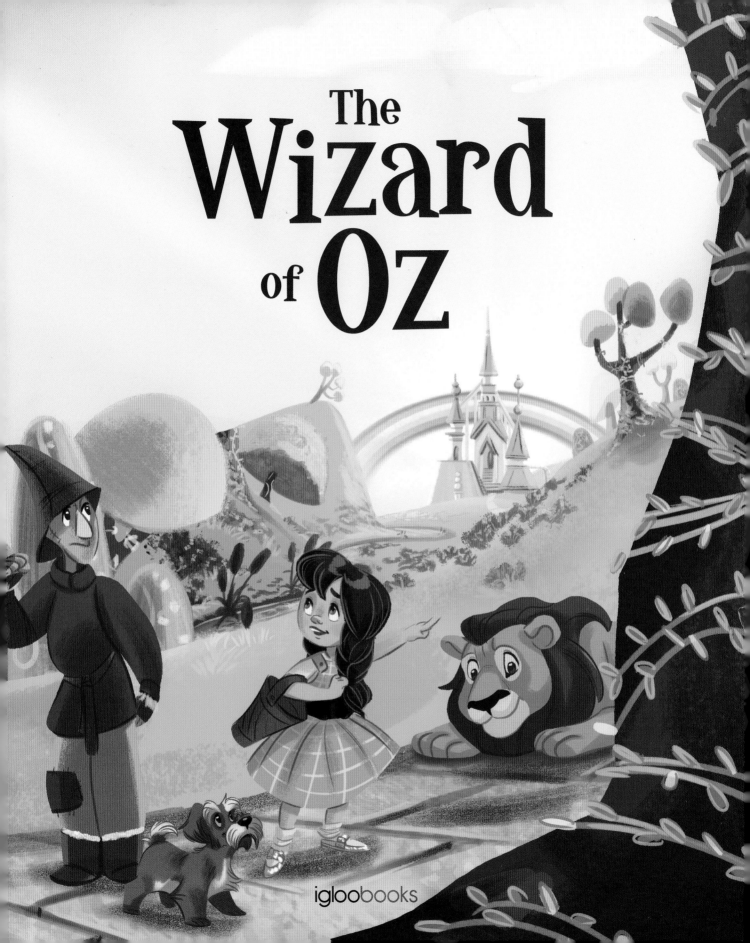

# The Wizard of Oz

igloobooks

Once, on the great Kansas prairies, a girl called Dorothy lived with her Uncle Henry, who was a farmer, Aunt Em, who was his wife, and a little dog called Toto. All around the farmhouse where they lived, as far as the eye could see, was flat, dry, sunbaked earth.

One day, a fierce wind came **swirling** from the North. **"Cyclone!"** cried Uncle Henry, running to get the cows from the field.

Dorothy grabbed Toto and dashed inside, but the little house **shook** and the terrible wind **lifted** it up as if it were as **light** as a **feather**.

The wind **wailed** and the house **swayed**. Hour after hour passed
and Dorothy grew so tired that she lay down and fell asleep.

Then, suddenly, the house landed with a

# THUD!

Jumping up, Dorothy flung open the door.
Outside wasn't the dry prairie,
but a beautiful land of tall,
colorful trees, sparkling streams,
and pretty flowers.

Out of the trees came a group of people who were the size of children, but looked like grown-ups.

**"Welcome to the land of the Munchkins,"** said a lady with a kind face. **"I am the Witch of the North. You have saved us from the Wicked Witch of the East."**

Dorothy's house had fallen on a witch! All that remained was a pair of silver shoes. "Oh, dear!" cried Dorothy. "I want to go home to Kansas."

"The Wizard of Oz will help you," said the Witch of the North. "Wear these shoes and follow the yellow brick road to the Emerald City. There, you will find the Wizard."

Dorothy put on the silver shoes and started on her journey. **"Come on, Toto,"** she said.

They had not gone far when they came upon a scarecrow in a field of golden corn.

**"Hello,"** said the Scarecrow. **"Where are you going?"**

**"To see the great Wizard of Oz,"** replied Dorothy.

**"Can he give me a brain?"** asked the Scarecrow, for he had a head full of straw.

**"I am sure he would,"** replied Dorothy, and they set off together.

Soon they came to a forest, where they found a man
made of tin. He was so rusty he could not move.

**"This oil will do the trick,"** said Dorothy, pouring it on the Tin Man's joints. She told him all about the journey to Oz.

**"I want to come, too,"** he said. **"I want the Wizard to give me a heart!"**

So Dorothy, the Scarecrow, and the Tin Man set off into the forest.

Suddenly, there was a ROAR as a lion bounded out of the trees.

Toto barked and the Lion opened his mouth as if to bite him. **"Don't you dare bite poor little Toto!"** cried Dorothy, slapping the Lion on his nose. **"You're just a big coward."**

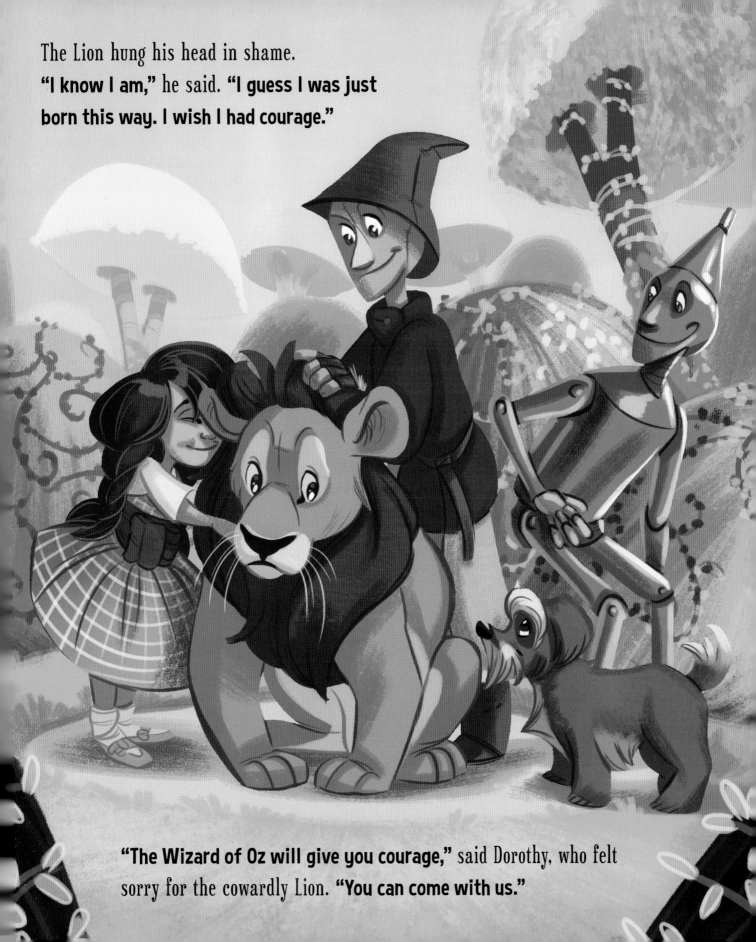

The Lion hung his head in shame. "I know I am," he said. "I guess I was just born this way. I wish I had courage."

"The Wizard of Oz will give you courage," said Dorothy, who felt sorry for the cowardly Lion. "You can come with us."

The little group walked for a very long time. At last, they came to a meadow full of poppies. Almost at once, Dorothy and the Lion fell asleep, for the scent of the flowers was poisonous.

**"We must move them or they will die,"** said the Tin Man. **"But the Lion is too heavy."** **"Now we shall never get to Oz,"** said the Scarecrow.

Then, just by chance, the queen of the field mice came by. She ordered her mice subjects to carry the Lion, while the Tin Man carried Dorothy.

Soon, Dorothy and the Lion were awake again.

**"Thank you, your Majesty,"** they said.

The friends traveled on, and at last they came to the gates of the **dazzling** Emerald City. Everything was green. The houses were green. There was green candy and popcorn, as well as green shoes, green hats, and green clothes of all sorts. Even the people were green!

The Guardian of the Gates led them through the streets until they came to a big building, exactly in the middle of the city. This was the palace of the great Wizard.

**"These visitors wish to see Oz, the Great and Terrible,"** announced the Guardian.

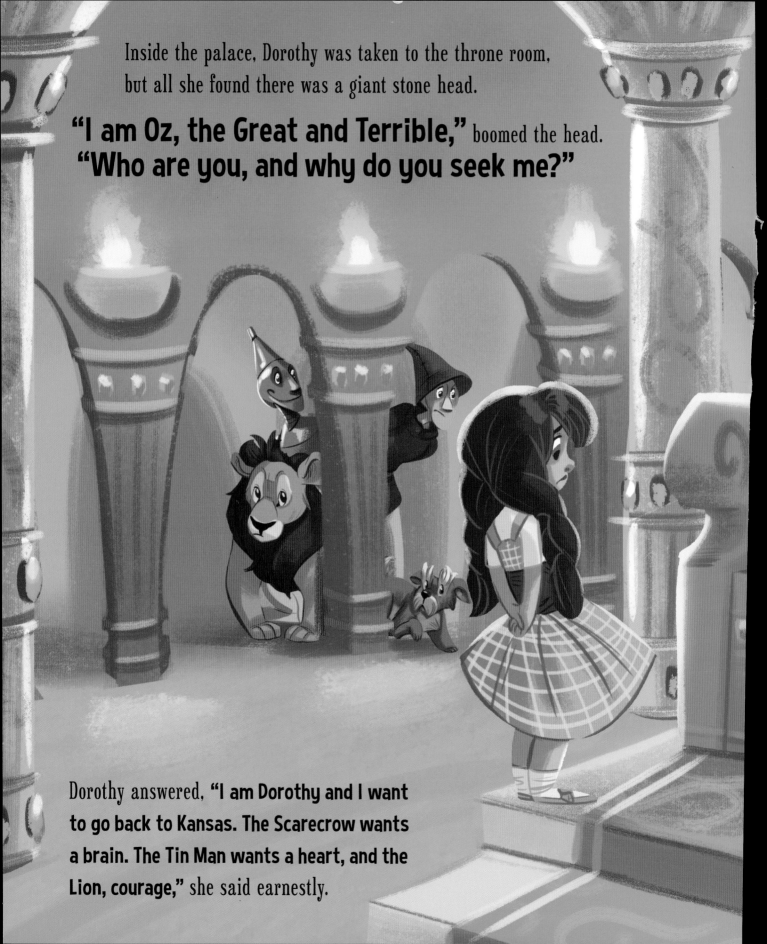

Inside the palace, Dorothy was taken to the throne room, but all she found there was a giant stone head.

**"I am Oz, the Great and Terrible,"** boomed the head. **"Who are you, and why do you seek me?"**

Dorothy answered, **"I am Dorothy and I want to go back to Kansas. The Scarecrow wants a brain. The Tin Man wants a heart, and the Lion, courage,"** she said earnestly.

"I shall grant all of these wishes
if you kill the Wicked Witch of
the West," said the voice.

Dorothy did not want to kill the
Witch, but knew that she must.

Now, the Wicked Witch of the West could see great distances. She saw Dorothy and her friends approaching and blew her magic whistle.

The sound sent crows, wolves, and bees to torment the travelers, but they managed to fight them all off.

The Witch was so **furious** that she sent winged monkeys to capture Dorothy and the Lion. The Lion was imprisoned in a cage and Dorothy became the Witch's servant. But what the Wicked Witch really wanted was Dorothy's silver shoes, for she knew they had great power.

No matter how hard the Witch tried to force Dorothy to obey her, though, she would not. So, as punishment, the Witch refused to feed the poor, imprisoned Lion.

After many days, Dorothy became so angry that she **threw** water over the Witch.

"What have you done?" screamed the Witch angrily. "Now I shall melt awaaaaay!"

The Witch did melt and soon disappeared altogether.

Dorothy quickly freed the Lion and, with the Scarecrow and Tin Man, returned at once to the Wizard's palace.

When the group reached the palace's throne room, they heard a loud voice say,
**"Who are you and why do you seek me?"**
**"Where are you?"** asked Dorothy. **"We cannot see anyone!"**

ROAR went the Lion, scaring Toto, who knocked over a screen.

Behind it was a small, gray-haired old man.

"I am the Wizard," said the old man sheepishly, his voice trembling. "I will do anything you ask."

"Keep your promises!" cried Dorothy sternly.

The Wizard gave the Scarecrow a brain, the Tin Man a heart, and the Lion, courage. However, he did not have the power to send Dorothy back to Kansas.

"We can go in a balloon," said the Wizard. "That is how I came to Oz." The Wizard busied himself making a big balloon and soon it was ready.

Just as it was about to take off, Toto ran away and Dorothy chased after him. **"Hurry!"** cried the Wizard . . .

. . . but the balloon floated away.

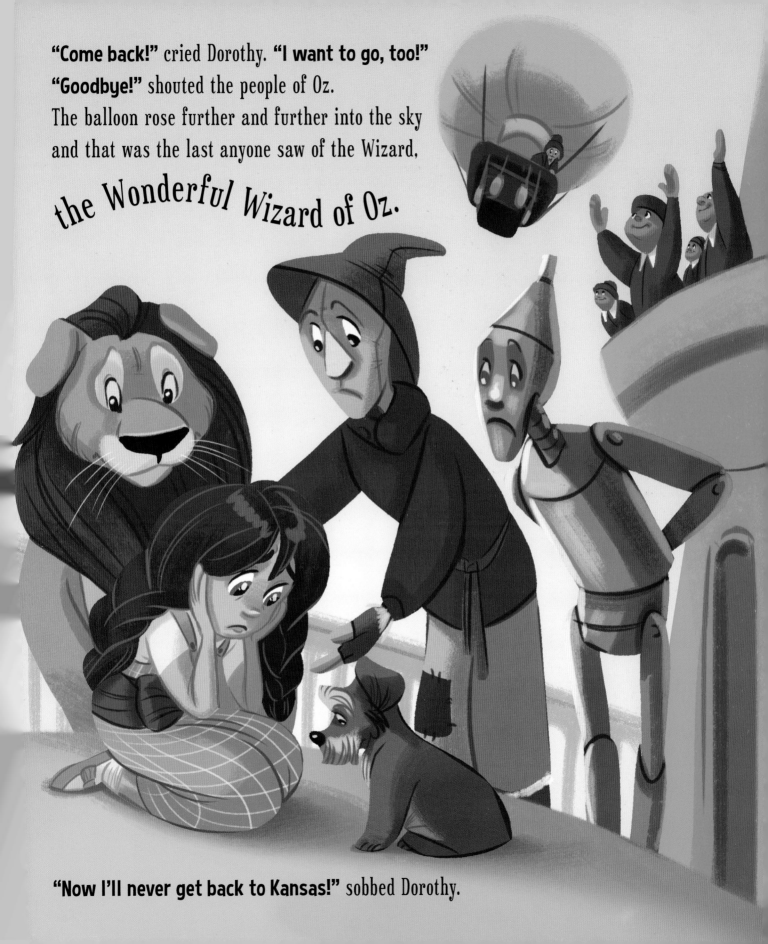

"Come back!" cried Dorothy. "I want to go, too!"
"Goodbye!" shouted the people of Oz.
The balloon rose further and further into the sky
and that was the last anyone saw of the Wizard,
the Wonderful Wizard of Oz.

"Now I'll never get back to Kansas!" sobbed Dorothy.

**"Glinda, the Witch of the South, may help,"** said the Scarecrow. **"The road to her castle is dangerous, but she is your only hope of getting home, Dorothy."**

So once again, the friends set off . . .

. . . through **enchanted** forests . . .

. . . where the trees seemed to come alive and **fierce** creatures lurked.

At last, they reached Glinda's castle.

"How can I help you, my child?"
asked the beautiful Witch.

"My greatest
wish is to get
back to Kansas,"
said Dorothy.

Glinda smiled. "Just knock the heels of your shoes
together three times and say where you wish to go."

Dorothy hugged and kissed her friends, and said a tearful goodbye.
**"Do not worry about us,"** said the Scarecrow, **"for we shall be very happy in Oz."**

Dorothy held Toto and **clicked** her heels three times. **"Take me home to Aunt Em!"** she cried.

Instantly, she was **whirling** through the air . . .

. . . until, suddenly, she landed with a big **bump** on the ground. **"I'm in Kansas!"** she cried, looking around.

Aunt Em was running toward her. **"My darling child. Where did you come from?"** she asked, covering the little girl in kisses. **"From the Land of Oz,"** said Dorothy. **"Oh, Aunt Em! I'm so glad to be home again!"**

Here ends the story of the
Wonderful Wizard of Oz.

# Discover three more enchanting classic tales. . . .

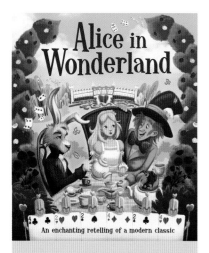

### Alice in Wonderland

An enchanting retelling of a modern classic

Join Alice and tumble down the rabbit hole into Wonderland, where nothing is as it seems. This beautiful book is perfect for creating the most magical of storytimes for every little reader.

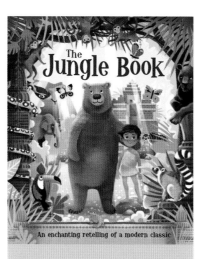

### The Jungle Book

An enchanting retelling of a modern classic

Join Mowgli as he learns the strange ways of the jungle, ever guided by the wise bear, Baloo. This retelling of the timeless classic, with beautiful illustrations, will capture every child's imagination.

### Treasure Island

An enchanting retelling of a modern classic

Set sail on a rip-roaring adventure in this classic story of swashbuckling pirates and hidden treasure. This exciting tale, with stunning original illustrations, is perfect for a thrilling storytime.

Look out for these other exciting tales in our storytime series!

igloobooks

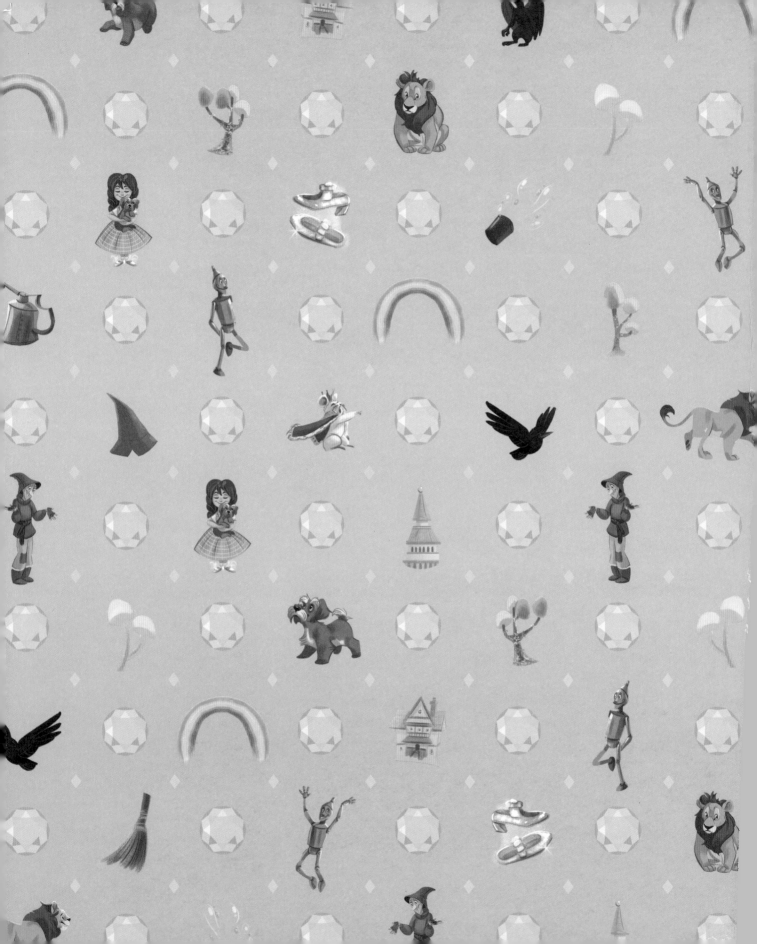